.010

To Grace -
welcome to the
world!
♡ Sarah, James + Owen S.Ket

Curse
in
reverse

For Conor and Matthew
—T. C.

For Oonagh Carroll-Warhola
—D. Z.

Atheneum Books for Young Readers
New York London Toronto Sydney Singapore

Once upon a time, an old witch named Agnezza visited the small village of Humburg. She had walked for miles over icy mountains and through snowy forests, and was tired, cold, and hungry.

As darkness fell over the village, Agnezza was drawn to the warm lights of Mrs. Ragg's snug cottage. She knocked, and Mrs. Ragg peered out.

"Please, missus," Agnezza asked, "may I have a bed for the night?"

Mrs. Ragg ran an inn and had four free beds. However, she did not like witches. "No," she replied. "There is a barn down the road for your type. Do not bother me again." She slammed the door shut.

Agnezza grew very angry. "I curse you!" she screeched. "I give you the Curse of the Silent Night!" And she spit on Mrs. Ragg's door.

Agnezza next tapped the large brass knocker on the double doors of Mr. Fooss.

"Please, sir," Agnezza asked, "may I share the warmth of your hearth tonight?"

Mr. Fooss had a grand house with four blazing fireplaces.

But he did not like witches either. “No,” he replied. “You are very dirty and you smell. Go away.” He shut the door in her face.

Again, Agnezza grew very angry. "I curse you!" she screeched. "I give you the Curse of the One-eyed Jack!" And she spit on Mr. Fooss's door.

Then Agnezza knocked on the thin door of Mr. and Mrs. Tretter. "Hello?" they answered together.

"Please," Agnezza asked, "may I share a crumb of your supper tonight?"

The Tretters had a simple one-room house. The furnishings were poor, but the home was rich in delicious smells. "Come in," they said.

The Tretters led Agnezza to the kitchen table. They gave her hot corn muffins with butter and fat, sizzling sausages to eat, and warm milk to drink. After she had eaten her fill, the Tretters dragged their only bed next to the fire for Agnezza to sleep in.

"But you have no place to sleep yourselves," protested Agnezza.

"It is only one night on the floor," said Mr. Tretter. "And you are our guest." With that, the Tretters said good night.

Agnezza slept well. She awoke to the smells of apple bread and strong coffee. It was a cold day, but sunshine poured through the window. As she shared breakfast with the Tretters, Agnezza said, "You keep a tidy home. But it is too tidy. And it is too quiet. Have you no children?"

“Alas,” said Mrs. Tretter, “we have not been so blessed.”

“’Tis a pity,” Agnezza said. “I too have no children. And you see how I live in my old age.” She shook her head and grumbled into her coffee mug.

Before she left, Agnezza turned to Mr. and Mrs. Tretter with a sad face. “You are very kind,” she told them. “I have nothing to give you. Therefore I give you a curse. I give you the Curse of the One-armed Man.” Agnezza turned away quickly and went down the frosty path.

The Tretters were amazed, and very hurt. Why did the witch curse them? They shut the door with furrowed brows and troubled hearts.

The Christmas season soon arrived, and Mrs. Ragg remembered the Curse of the Silent Night. She did not believe in curses. But she took no chances. On Christmas Eve, Mrs. Ragg locked her doors and windows. When Christmas carolers knocked on her door and sang "Silent Night," she threw rotten eggs at them. The carolers ran away. They sang "Silent Night" at church, but Mrs. Ragg did not go to church. Christmas Day passed. Nothing happened. Mrs. Ragg was relieved. The curse was not real.

Then on New Year's Day a knight in armor of rusted steel rode into the village upon a large, shaggy horse. A blizzard blew from the north. He came directly to Mrs. Ragg's inn and tapped on her door with his lance. Mrs. Ragg stepped out into the bitter air.

"Good day, Sir Knight," Mrs. Ragg greeted him. The knight stared at her, but did not speak.

Mrs. Ragg frowned. "I said, 'Good day, Sir Knight!' Have you no tongue?"

The knight pointed to his neck and shook his head wordlessly.

"Oh. Well, then. Are you looking for a room?" Mrs. Ragg asked.

The knight nodded wearily. Then he threw down a worn money pouch. A few pieces of silver spilled from it. Mrs. Ragg's eyes glittered.

"My home is your home," Mrs. Ragg said eagerly. "Stay as long as you want."

The knight slid off his horse. He brushed past Mrs. Ragg and stumbled inside.

Ye Olde Inn

Mrs. Ragg turned to follow. The door slammed in her face. Mrs. Ragg pounded on the door.

"Let me in, Sir Knight! Let me into my home!" she called angrily.

But the knight did not let her in. For the rest of the winter, he stayed snug in the inn, while Mrs. Ragg shivered and counted her cold silver pieces in the barn down the road.

Mr. Fooss heard about Mrs. Ragg and the Curse of the Silent Knight. He was worried. His was the Curse of the One-eyed Jack, and Mr. Fooss was very fond of card games and gambling. Surely the curse would bring misfortune at the card table.

So Mr. Fooss attended no card games. His friends begged him to join them at the card table. Mr. Fooss was tempted. But he stayed at home and played piano in his grand, warm house. He burned every deck of cards in the place. No, he would not fall to the Curse of the One-eyed Jack!

One day, as Mr. Fooss stepped outside his door, he heard a thunderous *crack*. Then, like the fist of God, a massive evergreen tree fell onto the roof of his house. *KER-WHOOMP!* The windows exploded and two of his walls collapsed. Mr. Fooss looked inside. His piano and fine furniture were matchsticks. His roof and chimneys were gone.

A giant lumberjack with a thick, black beard and a patch over one eye came up to Mr. Fooss.

"Did you do this?" Mr. Fooss asked furiously.

The lumberjack scratched his chin. "Yeah. Sorry about that. A bad aim. Me bad eye, y'know." The big man shrugged his shoulders. "Too late now."

"Who are you?" demanded Mr. Fooss.

The lumberjack grinned. "Call me Jack. One-eyed Jack."

Mr. and Mrs. Tretter were very worried. They had heard about the terrible curses that befell Mrs. Ragg and Mr. Fooss. Were they next?

Everywhere they went they watched carefully for a one-armed man.

Once, Mrs. Tretter saw a one-armed man at the market. She went straight home and locked the door.

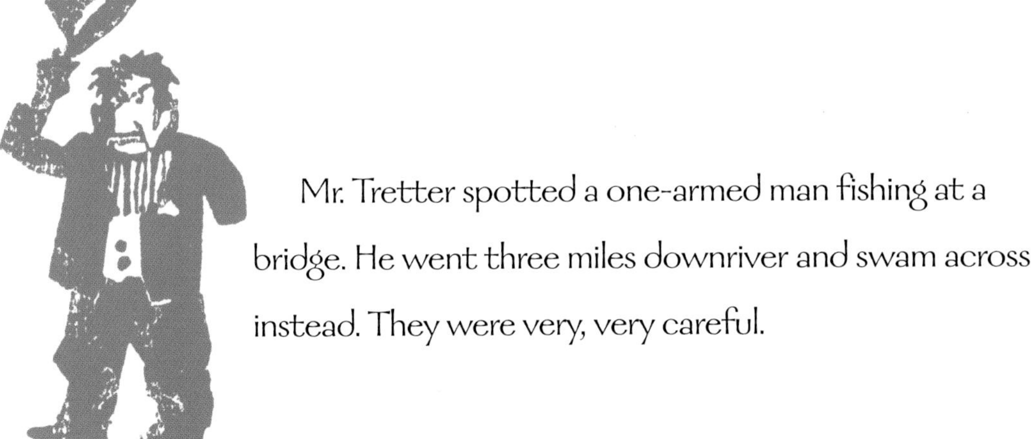

Mr. Tretter spotted a one-armed man fishing at a bridge. He went three miles downriver and swam across instead. They were very, very careful.

Soon great joy entered the Tretter home. A baby boy was born to them on an August day. Mr. Tretter danced in the streets and gave food and drink to all his neighbors.

"This is a surprise," said the village tailor. "I thought you could not have children."

"God blessed us," said Mr. Tretter.

"And the witch Agnezza cursed you," hissed Mrs. Ragg. "You surely tempt fate with your celebration."

Mr. Tretter turned pale. He quietly went inside and danced no more that day.

A year passed. Still the Tretter family suffered no ill luck. Their son grew in health and strength. Then one day, as Mr. Tretter attended the baby alone, a knock came on the door. Mr. Tretter opened it.

"May I have a crumb of your supper tonight?" asked Agnezza the witch.

Mr. Tretter was frozen with fear. But he said, "Yes, come in. Take a seat." He clutched his son close to his chest.

"Excuse me," said Mr. Tretter, "but I have work to do."

Agnezza watched as he held the baby and prepared supper.

He chopped vegetables with one hand.

Then he scooped them into the pot with one hand.

He filled the pot with water.

He hung the pot over the fire.

And then, still using one hand, he fed the fire with more wood.

To Agnezza's surprise, Mr. Tretter suddenly fell on his knee before her. "Please," he begged, "remove your curse. We live all our days in fear of the One-armed Man."

Agnezza laughed. "It is too late. The curse is done."

"Why?" asked Mr. Tretter angrily. "Why place a curse on our heads? We did you no harm. We gave you food and drink and a bed by the fire."

"Yes," agreed Agnezza, "and your hospitality deserved a blessing. However, I cannot bless you. I am a witch, not a priest. So I cursed you, with a curse in reverse."

"I do not understand," said Mr. Tretter.

"Do you not see? *You* are the One-armed Man."

Mr. Tretter then realized that Agnezza was right. With the baby in his left arm, he could use only his right arm to work. The curse had given them a son.

Mrs. Tretter arrived home and her husband told her everything. "It is a most wonderful curse!" Mrs. Tretter agreed. They all together laughed and danced with joy.

The Curse of the One-armed Man brought the Tretters three more children. And to the end of her years Auntie Agnezza was a welcome guest.